David Elliott

Romanism

Anatiposi

David Elliott

Romanism

Reprint of the original, first published in 1872.

1st Edition 2023 | ISBN: 978-3-38214-758-7

Anatiposi Verlag is an imprint of Outlook Verlagsgesellschaft mbH.

Verlag (Publisher): Outlook Verlag GmbH, Zeilweg 44, 60439 Frankfurt, Deutschland
Vertretungsberechtigt (Authorized to represent): E. Roepke, Zeilweg 44, 60439 Frankfurt, Deutschland
Druck (Print): Books on Demand GmbH, In de Tarpen 42, 22848 Norderstedt, Deutschland

(No. 151.)

ROMANISM

THE

Enemy of Civil Liberty.

BY THE

Rev. DAVID ELLIOTT, D.D.

PHILADELPHIA:

Presbyterian Board of Publication,

No. 1334 Chestnut Street.

ROMANISM

THE ENEMY OF CIVIL LIBERTY.

BY THE

Rev. DAVID ELLIOTT, D.D.

———

PHILADELPHIA:

PRESBYTERIAN BOARD OF PUBLICATION,

1334 CHESTNUT STREET.

WESTCOTT & THOMSON,
Stereotypers and Electrotypers, Philada.

ROMANISM

THE ENEMY OF CIVIL LIBERTY.

In view of the large influx of Roman Catholics into our country, and the activity of their priesthood in propagating their principles, and the injurious influence of their system upon the liberties of the country, serious apprehensions have been excited in the minds of many, and the question is often asked, *"Is the system of Romanism opposed to civil liberty?"*

This is certainly a question in which every American has a deep interest. It is admitted that we are the freest people on earth. We live in the enjoyment of civil liberty in its fullest extent. This is a great blessing conferred upon us by the God of heaven—a rich legacy bequeathed to us by our fathers.

Among intelligent and reflecting portions of the community, it is also highly appreciated and jealously guarded. This is right. It ought to be so. Take away a man's liberty, and you might almost as well take away his life. Prevent him from worshiping God according to the dictates of his conscience, and you crush his very being, and deprive him of that to which he has a moral and indefeasible right, and without which life is scarcely a blessing. Whatever system, therefore, whether religious, ecclesiastical or social, can be shown to be in conflict with the enjoyment of civil or political liberty, or whose legitimate tendency is in that direction, ought to be looked upon with dread and rejected as dangerous.

In the remarks which I am about to submit, my object will be to show that the system of Romanism, or the Roman Catholic system, as it is usually called, is hostile to civil liberty, and that for this reason, as well as others, it ought to be opposed and counteracted by all legitimate moral and religious efforts.

But let me not be misunderstood here. I do not mean to affirm that all Roman Catholics are the enemies of civil liberty. Many of them, no doubt, are its steadfast friends and advocates. But what I affirm is, that the Roman Catholic system of religion and of ecclesiastical law is at variance with civil liberty, and wherever it has been allowed to operate according to its true character it has proved destructive to its enjoyment. It is *the system*, therefore, against which we war, and not against individuals, who either may be ignorant of its true character or not feel themselves bound by its authority.

In approaching the proof of our position it may be proper, also, to remark that, if we can show that the Roman Catholic Church at any period of her existence—much more if at different periods of her existence—has authoritatively established and practically sanctioned doctrines or acts which are at

1 *

variance with civil liberty, we have gained our point; although, at other periods, she may not have assumed the same antagonistic attitude. For it will be carefully recollected that the Church of Rome claims to be *infallible*. What she once is she always is. What the pope affirms once she always affirms. What her councils decree once they always decree. As Dr. Doyle told the Protestant clergy of Ireland, *"Causa finita est."* The cause is finished. The question is settled. The Council of Trent has decided, and there can be no rehearing, and, of course, no reversal. The admission of change would be destructive of infallibility. Hence the decisions of her popes and councils, whenever and wherever made, are always binding. And although, in the days of her weakness, she may connive at their infraction, whenever she recovers her power she will enforce them, if need be, by the penal sanctions of the sword and the fagot.

That we may perceive with greater distinctness the opposition of Romanism to civil liberty, it may be proper to state wherein civil liberty consists.

Without attempting a minutely exhaustive definition, we may safely affirm that civil liberty consists eminently in *security against all encroachments on our natural and conventional rights, and in freedom from individual restraint, further than may be necessary for the general good.* Where this security does not exist, there is no true liberty.

Now, we affirm that Romanism is hostile to civil liberty, because it subverts and destroys the foundations of all security in the enjoyment of civil and political privileges. This it does in various ways, some of which I will now proceed to point out.

1. It does so *by denying men the free and unrestrained use of the Bible, which teaches them the knowledge of their rights and inculcates that moral virtue which is necessary to their preservation.* The Bible is the great text-book of civil liberty. Its instructions

furnish the best possible security against all encroachments on the rights of men. To "love our neighbor as ourselves" is the fundamental law of the Bible in reference to this point. And its great practical rule of social and political ethics is, "All things whatsoever ye would that men should do to you, do ye even so to them; for this is the law and the prophets." (Matt. vii. 12.) It not only denounces and condemns all injustice and oppression in general, but it specifically enjoins upon rulers and people the right and equitable discharge of their respective duties, so that there may be no oppression on the one hand, nor any encroachment on the exercise of lawful authority on the other. Its language is, "He that ruleth over men must be just, ruling in the fear of God." (2 Sam. xxiii. 2, 3.) "When the righteous are in authority, the people rejoice; but when the wicked beareth rule, the people mourn." (Prov. xxix. 2.) On the other hand, the injunctions in regard to submission to rightful authority are full and explicit. "Let every soul be subject unto the higher powers: the powers that be are ordained of God. Wherefore ye must needs be subject, not only for wrath, but also for conscience sake. Render, therefore, to all their dues; tribute to whom tribute is due; custom to whom custom; fear to whom fear; honor to whom honor." (Rom. xiii. 1.) This same apostle — Paul the aged—instructs Titus, a younger brother in the ministry, to "put them in mind to be subject to principalities and powers, to obey magistrates." (Tit. iii. 1.) Rebellion against lawfully constituted government is everywhere testified against in the Bible as a heinous offence.

These, and others of a similar kind, are the principles which give security to men in the enjoyment of their civil and political rights and privileges — authority equitably and righteously exercised, obedience conscientiously and promptly rendered, as that which is justly due. Where these principles are observed, there can be no encroachment, either of rulers or ruled, upon each others' rights. Nothing unjust will be demanded. Nothing that is justly due will be withheld. Every man's rights will be respected in the station which he occupies and in the relations which he sustains. Hence, the more familiar men are with the Bible, the more deeply will they be imbued with its principles, and the greater security will there be for the full and safe enjoyment of their civil liberties. The whole history of the Christian world proves this. Without going far back, where now does liberty hold its sway in its purest forms? Is it not in those nations where the Bible is most extensively circulated and read? where the people are most thoroughly indoctrinated in its principles, and most fully subject to its control? Compare Great Britain with Spain (before the late revolution) and Portugal, the United States with South America and Mexico, and the force of these remarks will be manifest.

Is not that system, therefore, the enemy of civil liberty which keeps the Bible from the people? which forbids its circulation, or allows it only subject to the censorship of those whose aggrandizement depends on its suppression? Such is the system of Romanism. It is opposed to the free circulation of the Bible without note or comment: to the unrestrained perusal of this great charter of civil and religious rights. For the truth of this allegation we appeal to facts. And here we may confidently refer to the authoritative canons of their own church.

The decrees of the Council of Trent are admitted by all true Catholics to be authoritative. This council was called by Pope Paul III. to meet at Trent, a city of the Tyrol, on the border of Italy, on March 15, 1545, but was not actually opened until the 13th of December following. By this council it was decreed that " No one, confiding in his own judgment, shall dare to wrest the sacred Scriptures to his own sense of them, contrary to that which hath been held and still is held by the Holy Mother Church, and whose right it is to judge of the true meaning and interpretation of sacred writ, or contrary to the unanimous consent of the fathers, even though such interpretation should never be published." This decree is incorporated in the creed of Pope Pius IV., published in December, 1564, and which has ever since been considered, in every part of the world, an accurate summary of the Roman Catholic faith. And to this creed every non-Catholic, on his admission to the Roman Catholic Church, is required publicly to testify his assent, " without restriction or qualification."

Before the adjournment of the Council of Trent, a committee was appointed to prepare an index of prohibited books. Not being prepared to report before the council adjourned, the matter was referred to the pope, under whose inspection the index was published in March, 1564. Among the rules prefixed to the index is the following, viz:

" It is manifest from experience that if the Bible, translated into the vulgar tongue, be indiscriminately allowed to every one, the temerity of men will cause more evil than good to arise from it."

Pope Clement XI., also, in his famous bull " Unigenitus," issued A. D. 1713, evinces the same decided hostility to the use of the Scriptures by the people, as the following fact demonstrates: Father Quesnel, a French priest, in a commentary on the New Testament, published A. D. 1699, had laid down, amongst others, the following proposition, viz. : " That it is useful and necessary, at all times, in all places, and for all sorts of persons, to study and know the spirit, piety and mysteries of the Holy Scripture; that the reading of the Holy Scripture is for everybody ; and that the Lord's day ought to be sanctified by Christians by reading pious books, and, above all, the Holy Scriptures." These propositions the pope in his bull condemns, and stigmatizes the whole as " false,

2

captious, shocking, offensive to pious ears, scandalous, pernicious, rash, seditious, impious, blasphemous."

In like manner, in the "Declaration of the Catholic Bishops, the Vicars Apostolic, and their coadjutators in Great Britain," we find them directly opposing the authorized reading and circulation of the Scriptures, as calculated to do much evil, and, among others, to lead into "*error and fanaticism in religion, and to seditions and the greatest disorders in states and kingdoms.*"

Pius VII., also, writing to Archbishop Gnezn in 1816, calls the Bible-society "a most crafty device by which the very foundations of religion are undermined, a pestilence, and defilement of the faith most imminently dangerous to souls." And Pope Leo XII., as late as the year 1824, speaking of the same Bible society, says that it "strolls with effrontery throughout the world, contemning the traditions of the holy fathers, and, contrary to the well-known decree of the Council of Trent, labors with all its might and by every means to translate, or rather to pervert, the Holy Bible into the vulgar languages of every nation: from which proceeding it is greatly to be feared that what is ascertained to have happened to some passages may also occur with regard to others, to wit, that by a perverse interpretation the gospel of Christ be turned into a human gospel, or, what is still worse, into the gospel of the devil."

With these views of the pope the Irish Roman Catholic prelates, to whom this was written, fully accorded; and they charged their flocks to give up to the priests the copies of the Scriptures they had received from the Bible societies, together with the publications of the Religious Tract Society. As an evidence that the Irish priests entered fully into the spirit of the pope, at a meeting at Carlow the next year (1825), at which the Rev. T. O'Connell and others were present, resolutions were passed denouncing the Bible as no sufficient rule of faith. They also pro-

claimed the right of private judgment to be a
" fertile source of fanaticism, error, dissen-
sion, and subversive of the peace of society ;"
asserting, also, that " Bible societies are nothing more than an exchequer for the levying of
taxes on the generosity and credulity of good
men, by idleness, ignorance and imposture."

In an examination, also, before a committee of the English House of Commons,
Bishop Poynter, the vicar apostolic, and Mr.
Charles Butler, two of the most enlightened
of the English Roman Catholics, gave it as
their opinion that it was contrary to Catholic
principles to allow the free use of the Bible
among the people, without notes and com-
ments.

These testimonies are amply sufficient to
prove that Romanism is opposed to the free
and unrestrained use of the Bible by the people. By its authoritative edicts and its official teaching, it deprives them of that which
is the best preservative and defence of civil
liberty—for the free use of the Bible, we

repeat it, is always favorable to civil liberty, and gives security to men in the enjoyment of their rights.   Of this we have a very strik- ing testimony in the declaration of the Jews in the city of New York, as reported in the winter of 1843.   Attempts had been made in that city by the Roman Catholics to exclude the Bible from the common schools, and they had so far succeeded as to secure a report from the fourth ward in favor of its exclusion.* During the discussions on the subject, it was alleged by some one that the Jews were

* The Roman Catholic Bishop Bayley, of New Jersey, in a letter to a Romish cardinal, assails the "public school system" as the source of most of the prevalent public and private dishonesty !   He also adds, that "It is the greatest enemy of the Catholic Church and of all dogmatic truth."

Archbishop McClosky, of New York, also asserts that, "So far as Catholic children are concerned, the workings of the public school system have proved and do prove highly detrimental to their faith and morals." This opposition to the "public school system" arises chiefly from its allowing the reading of the Bible by the pupils, or in their hearing.

2 *

opposed to its use in the public schools. To this, Colonel Stone, a prominent citizen, replied that he " had been called upon by a large number of most respectable and intelligent Jews, and among them Rabbi Isaacs, who requested him to state, among other things, that ' they were opposed to the fourth ward report (which was against the use of the Bible), because they *had enjoyed civil rights only in countries where there was a free circulation of the Bible.* In such countries only had they ever been permitted to enjoy civil rights in common with other religious denominations.'" This is a striking fact, and deserves to be remembered.

But we shall be told that the Bible is allowed to Roman Catholics. But how is it allowed? They are not at liberty to choose their own version, but they must take the Vulgate Latin, or the Douay and Rhenish translations, in which Dr. Whitaker tells us that Isodorus Clarius Brixianus reports no less than *eight thousand* errors. Then, the people must have the permission of their priest or confessor to read this, which permission is granted only to "those persons whose faith and piety they apprehend will be augmented and not injured by it." Then, they must read the Scriptures "according to the sense which the Holy Mother Church has held and does hold, to whom it belongs to judge of the true sense and interpretation of the holy Scriptures." And how the church judges in relation to civil rights and privileges, we shall see before we close this discussion. The truth is, that the Roman Catholic Church is the open and undisguised enemy of the free circulation of the sacred volume—the Bible. And hence it is that civil liberty withers at her approach and dies under her embrace. But, leaving this point, I proceed to observe:

2. That Romanism destroys men's security in the enjoyment of civil and political liberty, *by the unlimited and uncontrolled power which it vests in the hands of the pope.* It creates a despotism in the person of an individual

which is highly dangerous, if not destructive to the rights of men.

It is notorious that some of the most distinguished of the popes have claimed an absolute and universal power and control in temporal as well as in spiritual things. In the twenty-seven sentences of Gregory VII. and his council, called " Dictatus Papæ," it is declared " that the pope ought to be called the Universal Bishop; that his name alone ought to be recited in the church ; that he alone ought to wear the tokens of imperial dignity ; that all princes ought to kiss his feet ; that he is to be judged by none ; that he has power to depose emperors and kings," etc.

Pope Adrian IV. also—as Rapin, relying on the authority of Cambden, informs us—laid claim to the highest temporal sovereignty. Henry II. of England, being desirous to annex Ireland to his dominions, applied to the pope for his approbation. Accordingly, Adrian issued his bull, A. D. 1154, in which he uses the following language to the English

monarch : " It is certain, as you yourself
acknowledge, that Ireland, as well as *all other
islands* which have the happiness to be
enlightened by the sun of righteousness, and
have submitted to the doctrines of Christian-
ity, are *unquestionably St. Peter's right,* and
belong to the jurisdiction of the Roman
Church." And then, after giving Henry
leave to do what he thought best in the prem-
ises, and charging the people to submit to his
jurisdiction, he adds : " Provided always
that the rights of the Church are invariably
preserved, and the *Peter-pence* duly paid."
(This Peter-pence was a kind of yearly
tribute paid to the see of Rome, and levied
on every family in England.) The grant
thus made by Adrian was afterwards confirmed to Henry and his successors by Pope
Alexander III. In like manner Paul IV.,
on application of Philip and Mary, informed
their ambassadors that he had " erected Ireland into a kingdom, in virtue of apostolical
power."

Innocent III. also laid claim to the highest temporal powers. In his bull granting the kingdoms of England and Ireland to King John he says: "Jesus Christ the King of kings and Lord of lords, and priest according to the order of Melchisedek, hath so united the royal and sacerdotal power in the church, that the kingdom is but a royal priesthood, and the priesthood the royal power; and it hath pleased God so to order the affairs of the world, that these provinces, which had anciently been subject to the Roman Church *in spirituals*, were now become subject to it *in temporals*." This same pope asserted his presumptuous claims to the most absolute power, by telling Richard I. that *"he held the place of God upon earth*, and, without distinction of persons, he would punish the men and the nations that presumed to oppose his commands." Indeed, Boniface VIII. pronounces it to be "necessary to salvation that every human creature be subject to the absolute authority of the pope; that there are two swords in the power of the Church—the *spiritual* and the *material:* one in the hand of the pope, another which is in the hands of kings and warriors, *but whose exercise depends on the good pleasure and indulgence of the pope.*" *

So fully has this doctrine been recognized, that it has usually been deemed *heresy* in the Roman Catholic Church to deny the supremacy of the pope. This same Boniface VIII., in a letter to Philip IV., usually called "*The Fair*," king of France, employs the following language: " Boniface, bishop and servant of the servants of God, to Philip, king of France: Fear God and keep his commandments. We would have you to know that you

---

* A few days before the riot in New York, in July of 1871, the following declaration was put forth by the leading Roman Catholic paper in this country:

" *While the State has rights, she has them only in virtue and by permission of the superior authority, and that authority can only be expressed through the Church—that is, through the organic law—infallibly announced and unchangeably asserted, regardless of temporal consequences.*"

are subject to us, both in things spiritual and temporal, and we declare all those *heretics* who believe the contrary." And in another place he says, " God hath established us over kings and kingdoms, to pluck up, to overthrow, etc." In like manner, Pope Clement VI. declares that " The pontifical authority is not subject to the temporal or regal, *nor to any power on earth.*"

To this claim of universal dominion, and especially of temporal dominion, the royal pontiffs have most pertinaciously adhered. As an example of this, I would refer to what occurred in the reign of James the First of England. After the Gunpowder Plot, Parliament, for the discovery of popish recusants who refused to acknowledge the king's independent sovereignty, framed an oath of allegiance in which persons were required to acknowledge the king's sovereignty over the realm, and the power of the pope to depose him or dispose of his dominions was denied. Pope Paul V., however, issued a brief, dated

Oct. 31, 1606, forbidding the Catholics to take the oath. And in the second brief, the next year, he declared to them that, if they took the oath, "*they forfeited all hopes of salvation.*" Here you observe that, in a simple question of *temporal* sovereignty, the pope boldly claimed the pre-eminence, and a right to lord it over the king. And as stated by Rapin—from whom we quote—Cardinal Bellarmine seconded the claim of the pope, and wrote a book against the oath.

Such are some of the high claims and pretensions which have been made by many of the most prominent popes to absolute and universal authority, both spiritual and temporal. These high claims have also been sanctioned by councils, and advocated and defended by many of their most eminent men and standard writers. Thus, in the first Council of Lateran, A. D. 1512, under Julius II. and Leo X., Cajetan, Christopher, Marcelli, and many others, attributed to the pope this same unlimited power, with the appro-

bation of the council. Now, it is well known
that this Council of Lateran was approved
by the Council of Trent, and that the Council of Trent is received and acknowledged
as authoritative by nearly the whole Roman
Catholic world, so that these high claims of
the Roman pontiffs may be considered as
having received the sanction of the entire
Roman Catholic Church.

Their standard writers, too, such as Bellarmine, Baronius, Perron, and others, main-
tain the temporal authority of the popes, and
their right to excommunicate and depose
princes, as an article of the Catholic faith.
Bellarmine says, "That by reason of the
spiritual power, the pope, at least indirectly,
hath a supreme power even in temporal matters." He discourses on the whole subject in
the following manner: "The spiritual power
does not intermeddle with temporal things,
but suffers them all to go on as they did before they were united, provided they be no
hindrance to the spiritual end, and be not

necessary for attaining it. But, should any
such thing happen, the spiritual power may
and ought to confine the temporal by every
method that shall be judged necessary. He
(the pope) may change kingdoms, and take
them from one person to give them to another,
*as a sovereign spiritual prince, if that be neces-
sary for the salvation of souls.*" I need hardly
say that the authority of Cardinal Bellarmine in reference to the question before us
is great and controlling in the Church of
Rome. He was a counselor of the court of
Rome, wrote under the eye of the pope, ded-
icated his books to him, and, as a token of
his approval of his labors, he was rewarded
by his Holiness with a cardinal's hat.

Thomas Aquinas, known by the name of
"The Angelical Doctor," teaches the same
doctrine. He affirms that *"In the pope is
the top of both powers*, and by plain consequence asserting that, when any one is excommunicated for apostasy, his subjects are
immediately freed from his dominion and

their oath of allegiance to him." Baronius, too, a cardinal, and who would have been pope but for the opposition of the Spanish court, says that "There can be no doubt of it but that the civil principality is subject to the sacerdotal, and that *God hath made the political government subject to the dominion of the spiritual Church.*"

The popes did not rest satisfied with setting up these high claims to temporal power, but they carried them out in practice. Thus, Innocent III. actually deposed Otho IV., emperor of Germany, A. D. 1212. The most extraordinary and tyrannical measures were also adopted by this same pontiff in relation to King John of England. The pope and king had quarreled in consequence of the attempt of Innocent to force an archbishop into the see of Canterbury without the consent of the monarch. John proving refractory on his hands, the pope first laid the whole kingdom of England under an *interdict*, by which divine service was suspended in all the churches throughout the realm. Afterwards, he excommunicated the king, and freed his subjects from their oath of allegiance; and, finally, he deposed the haughty monarch and offered his kingdom to Philip Augustus, King of France. John, finding himself reduced to extremities, made his peace with the pope by tendering to him his crown, which the pope accepted, and after five days returned it. And what is worthy of special notice here is, that John subsequently—A. D. 1215—granted his subjects *Magna Charta*, which to this day is considered the foundation of English liberty, and having guaranteed its faithful observance by the sanction of an oath, the pope, in the exercise of his pontifical power, annulled the charter, released the king and his subjects from their oaths, and pronounced a "sentence of excommunication against every one who should persevere in maintaining such treasonable and iniquitous pretensions."

At a somewhat earlier period—A. D. 1076

3 *

—Gregory VII., commonly known by the name of Hildebrand, deposed Henry IV., emperor of Germany, in consequence of a quarrel on the subject of investitures. It may be interesting to some to see the form of deposition used on that occasion, which is as follows, viz.:

"For the dignity and defence of God's Holy Church, in the name of Almighty God, the Father, Son and Holy Ghost, I depose from imperial and regal administration King Henry, son of Henry, some time emperor, who too boldly and rashly hath laid hands on thy Church; and I absolve all Christians subject to the empire from that oath whereby they were wont to plight their faith unto true kings: for it is right that he should be deprived of dignity who doth endeavor to diminish the majesty of the Church."

This quarrel between Henry and the pope was attended with very serious results. "It is computed," says Hume, "that the quarrel occasioned no less than sixty battles in the reign of Henry IV. and eighteen in that of his successor, Henry V., when the claims of the sovereign pontiff finally prevailed." This bold and restless pontiff extended his usurpations all over Europe, and even beyond it. "He pronounced the sentence of excommunication against Nicephorus, emperor of the East; he degraded Boleslas, king of Poland, from the rank of king, and even deprived Poland of the title of a kingdom," and assumed and exercised other powers of the most tyrannical kind.

Pope John XXII. excommunicated the emperor Lewis of Bavaria, and absolved his vassals from their oath of fealty, and annulled all treaties of alliance between him and foreign princes. And Pope Pius V., by his bull—A. D. 1570—deprived Queen Elizabeth of England of her kingdoms, and absolved her subjects from their oath of allegiance. And in 1585 Pope Sextus V., in a bull against Henry, king of Navarre, afterward the great Henry IV. of France, and the prince of Conde, uses the following language: "We deprive them and their posterity for ever of their dominions and kingdoms;" also, "By the authority of these presents, we do absolve and set free all persons, as well jointly as severally, from any such oath, and from all duty whatsoever in regard of dominion, fealty and obedience, and do charge and forbid all and every of them that they do not dare to obey them, or any of their admonitions, laws and commands."

It would be easy to extend these examples of the exercise of pontifical tyranny in relation to the dethronement of civil rulers; but it may be sufficient to observe that the history of the Roman Catholic Church shows that above *sixty* princes have been excommunicated by upwards of *forty* popes. These examples prove, beyond controversy, what were the high claims and the settled doctrines and practices of the Roman Catholic Church in reference to the temporal power of the pope during those centuries in which

Romanism had the ascendency and most extensively prevailed.

But it is alleged by the apologists of Rome that this doctrine of the pope's power to dethrone rulers of states and kingdoms has become obsolete, and no longer exists. There are facts, however, in opposition to such an allegation, and which prove that the same doctrine is still held, and only waits a favorable opportunity for its practical development. Thus, as late as the year 1729, Pope Benedict XIII. re-canonized Gregory VII., the famous Hildebrand, who, in the two preceding centuries, had been placed among the saints by Gregory XIII. and Paul V. He moreover appointed an *office* in the Liturgy in honor of Hildebrand, to be celebrated on the 25th of May annually. In this office reference is had to his dethroning Henry and absolving his subjects from all duty toward him. This office, it is reported, is still celebrated in Italy, which shows conclusively that the same tyrannical and dangerous power is still claimed, and, if favorable opportunities were afforded, would doubtless be exercised.

But we have still more explicit evidence on this subject, in a letter addressed to the archbishop of Dublin by the apostolic nuncio at Brussels, Thomas Maria Ghilini, archbishop of Rhodes, bearing date the 4th of October, 1768. The subject of this letter is the oath abjuring the doctrine "that the pope has power to depose sovereigns and release subjects from their allegiance." "On many accounts," the nuncio says, "this new oath is blamable, and unworthy of Catholic prelates; but it is, moreover, *intolerable*, if we consider the *protestation* which is annexed to it, to wit: of abominating and detesting, from the heart, the doctrine which is therein declared to be abominable and pernicious." (That is, the doctrine that the pope has power to depose sovereigns and release subjects from their allegiance.) "This doctrine," he continues, "which is asserted in the oath to be detestable, is defended and maintained by very many Catholic nations, and hath very often been followed in its practice by the apostolic see. Wherefore, it cannot be that any Catholic shall declare it to be detestable and abominable, without the assertion incurring the character of a rash proposition, *false, scandalous, and injurious to the holy see.*" And he goes on to say that if any of them have taken the oath, it "being in its whole extent unlawful, is, in its nature, void and null, and of no effect, so that it cannot, by any means, bind or oblige consciences."

Now, is it not clear from these facts that there is no relinquishment of the claim of the Roman pontiffs to an absolute and universal power over the civil authorities in all nations, and to dispose of rulers and people according to their pleasure? And can civil liberty be secure under the operation and control of such a system as this? Can any government on earth be safe, when its continuance and action are dependent on the caprice of such men as Hildebrand or Innocent III.?   It cannot be.

I would further direct the reader's attention to another form in which this power of the pope has been applied to the detriment of civil liberty. By the 17th canon of the Council of Clermont, bishops and priests are forbidden to take the oath of fidelity to kings or to any layman. The Third Council of Lateran—A. D. 1179—with Pope Alexander III. at its head, forbids, under the pain of excommunication, "all laics from obliging ecclesiastics to appear before the judges;" thus exempting them from obedience to the civil power. The same council forbids the exaction of taxes from the clergy. And the Fourth Council of Lateran—A. D. 1215— with Innocent III. at its head, renewed this canon, and sentenced to excommunication all who offended against it. Boniface VIII. also published a constitution of like tenor, in which he avers that the laity have no power to tax ecclesiastics, and ordains the punishment of excommunication against all who shall pay such tax, or who shall impose it, whether they be kings, princes, magistrates or others. Thus, the pope and his councils claim and exercise an entire control over the civil power, to restrain and dispose of it as they please. Magistrates must not, in the discharge of their official functions, call ecclesiastics before them, nor attempt to impose on them any tax: nor, if this is done, must the clergy submit to such exactions, on pain of subjecting themselves to the severest penalties of the Church.

In the reign of Edward I. of England, in the thirteenth century, there is a very instructive piece of history, which strikingly exhibits the hostility of the pope to the principles of civil liberty. The encroachments of the papal power, during the reigns of John and Henry III., had drawn forth the complaints of the English against the Church of Rome. But the pope in his turn also

4

complained. In "The Collection of Public Acts," these complaints are found embodied in a bull of Pope Clement V. Among these complaints of the pope, one is, "*That clergymen were subjected to the trial of twelve lay persons, and were acquitted or condemned by the verdict of these twelve incompetent judges.*"

Here, you will observe, the pope quarrels with the "trial by jury," which, since the days of Alfred the Great, has ever been considered the great palladium of civil liberty: "an institution," as has been well remarked, "admirable in itself, and best calculated for the preservation of liberty and the administration of justice that was ever devised by the wit of man." Yet of this institution the pope complains as being an intolerable grievance, and claims that his clergy be delivered from it.

But, to come nearer home, even in our own country we have had an exemplification of the exercise of Romish ecclesiastical power, in regard to the right of property—a mere matter of secular interest. The facts to which we refer took place in the State of New York, in or about the year 1843. Bishop Hughes, the Roman Catholic bishop of that State, claimed that the property of the St. Louis Church, in the city of Buffalo, should be vested in him. To this the congregation demurred and refused to submit. As a punishment for their contumacy, the bishop withdrew from them their pastor, the Rev. Alexander Rex, and left them entirely destitute of pastoral care and without the enjoyment of the ordinances of religion. Now, what was this but the "interdict" of Innocent III. in miniature?—depriving the people of religious privileges to secure a concession in favor of his secular interests? And what makes it the more oppressive, in cases of this kind, is the fact that the only redress which the people have is through the pope, as by their canon law the authority of the bishop is necessary to give a priest the right to perform divine service in any of the churches in his diocese. So that even here, in this land of boasted freedom, the civil rights of men, in reference to their worldly property, are attempted to be superseded and wrested from them by ecclesiastical inflictions imposed upon them by the sworn officer and representative of the pope of Rome.

And is not this a constituent part of the system of Romanism? Undoubtedly it is. The pope, as we have seen from the teaching of Bellarmine, "has supreme power in temporal matters;" or, as Pope Innocent told Richard I., "*he holds the place of God upon earth.*" Of course, according to this doctrine, he has a right to any property he chooses to claim, and his bishops are bound to enforce his claim. For his bishops and clergy are required to swear "to be faithful and obedient to St. Peter and to the Holy Roman Church, and to our lord the pope, his successor, to receive and execute all his commands," etc.

In view of all these facts, which might be

easily multiplied, is it not evident that this doctrine of the pope's supremacy is highly dangerous to men's rights, and that the system of which it is an essential part is hostile to civil liberty? But on this part of the argument we cannot longer dwell, but pass on to observe,

3. That Romanism destroys men's security in the enjoyment of civil liberty, *by the loose and disorganizing character of its moral principles, which break down moral obligation, and subvert the very foundations of confidence and trust.*

The Roman Catholic Church teaches that faith is not to be kept with heretics, and by heretics she understands all who do not adhere to the Church of Rome. This doctrine, that faith is not to be kept with heretics, is abundantly sustained by the history of the Roman Catholic Church. Thus, Pope Martin V., in an epistle to Alexander, duke of Lythuania, says, "Be assured thou sinnest mortally if thou keepest faith with heretics."

4 *

On this same subject, Pope Gregory IX. en-
acted the following law, viz.: "Be it known
unto all who are under the jurisdiction of
those who have openly fallen into heresy, that
they are free from the obligation of fidelity,
dominion, and every kind of obedience to
them, by whatsoever mean or bond they are
tied to them, and how securely soever they
may be bound." And in the decretals of
this pope, the broad principle is laid down,
" That an oath disadvantageous to the Church
is not binding."

Of the same character is the doctrine of
Cardinal Perron and the French clergy.
After the murder of Henry IV., an oath
was proposed abjuring the doctrine that it
was lawful to assassinate kings, or depose
them for heresy, and absolve their subjects
from allegiance. Against this proposal the
clergy, with Cardinal Perron at their head,
remonstrated, declaring, " That if such a law
were established, they would entirely destroy
the communion which they had hitherto

maintained with all other churches; that such an oath could not be taken without acknowledging that the pope and the whole Church had erred, both in faith and in things pertaining to salvation." This doctrine of the clergy of France accords with that of Gregory IX., already recited.

Indeed, the general principle seems to have been fully settled in the Roman Catholic Church, that it is right to break public obligations for the benefit of the Church. Hence, popes and councils have acted on this principle. Thus, the pope persuaded Ladislaus, king of Hungary, to break the truce of ten years, made with Amurath, sultan of the Turks, and absolved him from the oath whereby it had been confirmed. And when Henry I. of England scrupled to break a promise he had made, Calixtus told him that "He was pope, and would absolve him from his promise." Henry II. also received a papal dispensation to violate his father's will, which he had sworn to observe.

A still more prominent illustration of this doctrine we have in the decree of the Council of Constance—A. D. 1415—on the subject of "the safe conduct" granted to heretics by temporal princes; especially in reference to the case of John Huss of Prague, the celebrated Bohemian Reformer. The decree runs thus: "The Holy Synod of Constance declares, concerning every safe conduct granted by the emperors, kings and other temporal princes to heretics, or persons accused of heresy, in hopes of reclaiming them, that it ought not to be of any prejudice to the Catholic faith or to the ecclesiastical jurisdiction, nor to hinder, but that such persons may and ought to be examined, judged and punished according as justice shall require, if these heretics shall refuse to revoke their errors, although they shall have come to the place of judgment relying upon their safe conduct, and without which they would not have come hither: and the person who shall have promised them security shall not, in this case, be obliged to keep his promise, by whatever tie he may have been engaged, when he has done all that is in his power to do."

Upon this decision of the council, Huss was condemned and burned, notwithstanding that he had come to Constance relying on the safe conduct given him by the Emperor Sigismund. Now, it is well known that the Council of Trent has confirmed the decrees of all the preceding general councils, and, consequently, that of Constance, which was held from 1414 to 1418 inclusive—something more than a century before that of Trent. Accordingly, in the creed of Pope Pius IV., which is a summary of the doctrines of the Council of Trent, the following is one of the articles to be professed, viz.: "I also profess, and undoubtingly receive, all other things delivered, defined and declared by the sacred canons and *general councils*, and particularly by the Holy Council of Trent." Indeed, the Council of Trent formally allows the violation of a solemn contract and oath in the case of a man who is betrothed to a woman, but who, before consummation, enters into religious orders. So that the Church of Rome, by her standard council, whose decisions all true Catholics acknowledge to be binding, has fully endorsed the doctrine that the most solemn promises and compacts may be violated for the benefit of the Church.

Nor is the conduct of the Council of Constance, in violating the safe conduct given to Huss, and putting him to death, approved only by the Roman Catholics of that period, but also by those of our own time. In proof of this, I refer to the " Eighth Report of the Commissioners of Irish Education Inquiry," printed by order of the House of Commons of Great Britain, as given by Lord Bexley in his address to the freeholders of the county of Kent, October 25, 1828. Examinations were instituted by these commissioners in relation to the doctrines held by leading Catholics who had charge of the education in institutions supported by government. Among others, the Rev. Dr. Crotty, president of Maynooth College, was examined touching the decree of the Council of Constance, which violated the safe conduct of Huss, which decree the doctor boldly justified, on the ground that Huss merited his fate by attempting to escape when he found he was to be burnt alive.

From the examinations, also, of Dr. Anglade, professor of moral theology, and of Dr. McHale his predecessor, it appears that in the text-book of the course of divinity used in the college, it is distinctly laid down that there is, in the Church, *a power of dispensing with oaths as well as with sins.*

In conformity with this doctrine, thus contained in their text-books and taught by their professors of theology, it was that Pope Clement VI. granted a special indulgence to King John and Queen Joan of France, and *to their heirs for ever*, that their confessors might commute, for such other works of piety as they might deem expedient, such *vows and oaths* as they had taken or might take in all time to come, and which they *might not profitably keep:* denouncing the wrath of Almighty God, and of his blessed apostles Peter and Paul, against all who should presumptuously attempt to alter this grant. The perfect absurdity of such a grant as this may divert the mind from its presumptuous wickedness. But when we reflect that this is only a practical exemplification of a doctrine belonging to their system, laid down in their standard books and taught in their halls of divinity, it assumes a more serious aspect, and ought to be looked upon with abhorrence, as highly detrimental to the civil and social interest of any community.

For what, now, I would ask, is the effect of this whole doctrine upon civil liberty and the rights of men? If the pope alone, or the pope and his councils together, have the power to annul contracts, to release men

from their official promises and oaths, to loose
the bonds which hold society together and
ensure its harmonious operation, what security
is there for the enjoyment of liberty or the
possession of any right? Suppose the pope,
having the power, should think it for the
benefit of the Church that the people of
these United States should be freed from
their obligation to obey the Constitution and
laws of the country, and so ordain; and suppose he should think it better not to execute
treaties, or fulfill contracts into which the
government has entered, and so order—who
would feel secure, or that his liberties were
safe? And would not all agree that such
assumptions of power, in dispensing with
moral obligations, were destructive of all
security in the enjoyment of any civil privilege? I doubt not but that every loyal
American citizen will thank God that the
pope has no such power in our country.
But if he had, may I not ask, after the fore-
going statements, whether the accredited prin-

5

ciples of Romanism would not authorize him to exercise it?

4. But I proceed to remark, further, that Romanism destroys men's security in the enjoyment of civil liberty *by its intolerant and persecuting character*. It may again be proper to say that we do not speak of individuals in the Roman Catholic Church, but we speak of their system, and of the workings of that system, as they have appeared in the past history of the Church and of the world. And here, again, we appeal to their own authorities in proof of what we have affirmed.

As has been already remarked, Bellarmine is admitted by Roman Catholics to be an orthodox expositor of their doctrines. He delivered his lectures in the college at Rome, by the appointment of Pope Gregory XIII., only fourteen years after the close of the Council of Trent, and on this account may be supposed to be well informed on the subjects treated, and to speak the very language

of his Church.   And what says Bellarmine
on the point now before us?   "Heretics," he
affirms, "are to be destroyed root and branch,
if that can possibly be done: but if it appear
that the Catholics are so few that they cannot, conveniently with their own safety, attempt such a thing, then it is best, in such a
case, to be quiet, lest upon opposition made
by the heretics the Catholics should be
worsted."

Again, he says, "It is not lawful for Christians to tolerate an infidel or heretical man,
if he endeavor to draw his subjects into his
heresy or infidelity; but it belongs to the
pope, to whom the care of religion is com-
mitted, to judge whether the king draws
them into his heresy or not.   It is therefore
the business of the pope to judge whether
the king should be deposed or not.   If the
Christians in former times did not depose
Nero, Diocletian, and Julian the apostate
. . . it was because they had not sufficient
power.   For that they had a right to do it

is evident from the apostle Paul, in his First
Epistle to the Corinthians, sixth chapter,
where he orders the Christians to establish
new judges of temporal affairs, that they
might not be obliged to carry their causes
before a judge who was a persecutor of Jesus
Christ. As they might establish new judges,
they might also choose new kings for the
same reason, if they had the power."

In accordance with this doctrine of Bellarmine, the bishops and clergy, in the oath of
allegiance to the pope which they are required to take, swear, among other things,
that they will "persecute and oppose all
heretics, schismatics and rebels to their sovereign lord the pope or his successors."
Hence, as a learned historian remarks, "All
clergymen of the Church of Rome, not born
within the verge of the ecclesiastical state,
are subjects of a foreign power, and bound
by the most sacred ties to lay violent hands
on all who profess a religion different from
their own."

The same intolerant doctrine is taught by the Council of Lateran, under Innocent III., A. D. 1215. The council, after declaring that they "excommunicate and anathematize all heresy, condemning all heretics, by what names soever they are called," add the following: "These, being condemned, must be left to the secular power to be punished." And, that there might be no flinching on the part of the secular powers, the same council provide that they are to be admonished and compelled to punish such offenders. To secure this, they must take the following oath, viz.: "That they will endeavor, *bona fide* and with all their might, to exterminate from every part of their dominions all heretical subjects universally that are marked out to them by the Church, so that from this time forward, when any one is promoted to any power, spiritual or temporal, he shall be obliged to conform to this. But if any temporal lord, being required and admonished by the Church, shall neglect to purge his

5 *

land from this heretical filthiness, he shall be tied up in the bond of excommunication by the metropolitan and his comprovincial bishops. And if he should neglect to make satisfaction within a year, it should be signified to the pope, that he might, from that time, pronounce the subjects absolved from allegiance to him, and expose his territories to be seized on by Catholics, who, expelling the heretics, shall possess without contradiction."

And, that Catholics might be encouraged in this work of persecution, it is added in the same chapter that "Catholics who, having taken the badge of the cross, shall set themselves to extirpate heretics, shall enjoy the same indulgence, and be fortified with the same privilege, as is granted to those who go to the recovery of the Holy Land."

As further proof of the persecuting character of popery, I would refer to the bull of Pope Innocent VIII. (the original of which is said to be in the library at Cambridge, England), which he issued for the extirpation of the Vaudois. This bull was given to Albert de Capitaneis, his legate and commissary general, for his expedition in the year 1487. In this document, which was the most fatal and notable of all the bulls against the Waldenses, he authorized his legate to call upon and receive all the archbishops, and bishops, and other brethren, with the inquisitor—"That they should take arms against said Waldenses and other heretics, and, with common counsels and means, crush and tread them as venomous serpents." He moreover entreated Charles, king of France, the noblemen of the kingdom, the confederates of Germany, and all the faithful, to "afford help to the said archbishops, bishops, etc., by suitable aids and by their secular arms, and that they vehemently and vigorously set themselves in opposition to these heretics, that so they may make them to perish, and entirely blot them out from the face of the earth." Such is a very brief outline of the substance of this famous bull. Its effects were of the

most desolating and horrible character, as it
is stated that, in consequence of it, not less
than eight hundred thousand of these Waldenses were destroyed.

Of a like intolerant character is the bull
of Pope Paul V., called *"in cona Domini,"*
dated April 4, 1613. To show what com-
prehensiveness of detail is included in this
remarkable document, I will quote part of
the first section, which commences as follows,
viz. : "We excommunicate and anathematize
in the name of God Almighty, Father, Son
and Holy Ghost, and by the authority of the
blessed apostles Peter and Paul, and by our
own, all Hussites, Wicklifites, Lutherans,
Zwinglians, Calvinists, Huguenots, Anabap-
tists, Trinitarians, and apostates from the
Christian faith, and all other heretics, by
whatsoever name they are called, and of whatsoever sect they be."

Every reader of history is familiar with
the *Edict of Nantes*, which was drawn up at
Nantes, A. D. 1598, by Henry IV. of France,

in favor of the Protestants. In this edict,
the liberty of worshiping God according to
the dictates of their own consciences was
granted to Protestants, and a full security
given for the enjoyment of their civil rights
and privileges, without persecution or molestation from any quarter. Through the insid-
ious arts of the priests and Jesuits, this edict
was revoked by Louis XIV. in 1685, in consequence of which the Protestants were deprived of the liberty of worshiping according
to their own convictions. And what added
to the grievance was, that the revocation was
followed by an express order to all the Re-
formed churches to embrace the Romish faith.
The effect of this was, that those who could
not leave the country were "assailed by every
barbarous form of persecution." And what
is worthy of notice in this connection is, that
although there had existed long and violent
quarrels between Louis and the pope, no
sooner had the king revoked the Edict of
Nantes than the pope wrote him a highly

complimentary letter, in which he extols him
for his "excellent piety," for having wholly
abrogated all those constitutions that "were
favorable to the heretics of his kingdom."

The same spirit of persecution is further
seen in the bull of Pope Urban VIII., dated
from the Vatican, May 25, 1643. This document was produced in the Court of the
King's Bench on the trial of Connor, Lord
Maguire, February 10, 1644. In this bull
the pope recites the great zeal of the Irish in
propagating the Christian faith, and endeav-
oring *by force of arms* to deliver their nation
from the oppressions of the heretics and to
extirpate the workers of iniquity, and then
grants them a full and plenary indulgence,
and absolute remission of all their sins, so
long as they should militate against said heretics and other enemies of the Catholic faith.

But we would fail of doing justice to our
argument on this part of our subject if we
did not refer to the *Inquisition*, as furnishing a
striking illustration of the intolerant and per-

secuting spirit of Romanism. This tribunal, dignified by the title of the "Holy Office," and of which the pope is the supreme head and lawgiver, was instituted against the Albigenses, by Pope Innocent III., in the early part of the thirteenth century, although he died before he succeeded in giving it permanent form. Its object was to search out heretics, to try and condemn them as enemies to the Romish faith, and thus to complete what "the preaching of missionaries, anathemas, crusades and wars could not fully accomplish." This tribunal soon "usurped a jurisdiction over the persons, lives and fortunes of men independent of the civil authority, to which they left nothing but the drudgery of executing their iniquitous acts." And, although in its institution it was only proposed to punish the crime of heresy, the inquisitors were vested with power to pursue and bring to confession all who were *suspected;* hence, assuming that those who were guilty of certain crimes against the civil law must be guilty of heresy, multitudes were thrown under suspicion, and arraigned and tortured for the purpose of bringing them to confession of their guilt. Its officers, called "familiars," were everywhere dispersed throughout the country. Whoever was suspected was addressed in the name of the Holy Inquisition, and, whether it were father or mother, son or daughter, brother or sister, husband or wife, they must be given up, without a murmuring word or any attempt to have them released. The proceedings respecting them were all of the most secret character, and the tortures they underwent were shocking to the sensibilities of the human heart.

How opposite all this is to the enjoyment of civil liberty needs no argument to prove. The mere statement of the facts is sufficient to show that a system which authorizes such a tribunal—one so tyrannical and irresponsible—must be adverse to the liberties of any country. It conflicts with the liberty of conscience and the free exercise of

our opinions and privileges, and places all at
the sovereign disposal of the pope and his
sworn emissaries.

Before closing this discussion, we have some
facts of a more recent date which we desire to
present, for the purpose of showing that this
doctrine of intolerance and persecution is still
held by the Roman Catholic Church.   As
late as the year 1808, Pope Pius VII. addressed a circular to all the cardinals in relation to the alterations made by Napoleon Bo-
naparte in the Gallican church.   This circular
contains the following passage in reference to
these alterations, viz. : "It is proposed that
all religious persuasions should be free, and
their worship publicly exercised ; but *we have
rejected this article as contrary to the canons
and councils of the Catholic religion,* to the
tranquillity of human life, and to the welfare
of the state."   It will be observed here that
one of the grounds on which the pope rejected
the proposed freedom of all religious denominations to enjoy their own modes of worship

6

was, that it was "contrary to the canons and
councils of the Catholic religion"—thus rec-
ognizing the validity of the old enactments
of the Church against heretics, and showing
that on this subject she remains the same that
she always was. The pope of 1808 cannot
consent that all religious persons shall have
liberty to worship God publicly and without
molestation, according to their own views,
*because it is contrary to the canons and decrees
of his Church!*

Still later, in the latter part of the year
1823, the Rev. Dr. Doyle, Roman Catholic
bishop of Kildare, Ireland, published "a
vindication of the principles of the Irish
Catholics," which was intended to conciliate
opposition and to place popery in the most
favorable light. In this publication he says,
"*Religious intolerance is a species of intolerance distinct in itself; it would appear to be
one of the first consequences following from the
idea of a divine revelation*" * — the amount

* As late as the early part of the year 1867, the Ro-

of which statement appears to be this: that, while he admits the intolerance of the Church and the existence of a divine revelation, he assumes it as a necessary corollary, from the infallibility of the revelation, that the Roman Catholic Church, which is infallible, may enforce its reception, as interpreted by her, by temporal penalties or physical coercion. Such appears to be the logic by which the bishop attempts to prove the divine right of the Roman Catholic Church to burn heretics or to deprive them of the privilege of worshiping God according to the dictates of their own consciences. And having laid down this proposition, he proceeds to ask, "What can influence the bulk of mankind, ignorant and stupid as they are, but

man Catholic paper of St. Louis, Mo., the organ of the archbishop of that city, uses the following ominous language, viz.: "*The Church is, of necessity, intolerant.* Heresy she endures when and where she must, but she hates it, and directs all her energies to its destruction. If Catholics ever gain an immense numerical majority, religious freedom in this country is at an end."

authority? What can preserve the Christian world from relapsing into the errors and impieties from which Christ has redeemed it but authority? What preserves unity in any church or state in the universe but authority? What fills, at the present day, these islands [England and Ireland] and Germany with the most frantic opinions, but *the want of an authority sufficient to coerce them?*" So that, according to this liege subject and sworn officer of the pope of Rome, it would be a most desirable consummation if they possessed sufficient authority and power to coerce the Protestants of Great Britain and Germany to give up their frantic opinions on the subject of religion. And no doubt it would be equally gratifying to this benevolent bishop to be enabled to exercise the same authority in regard to the Protestant citizens of the United States.

But it may be interesting to come a little nearer to our own time, and to learn the opinions of Pope Gregory XVI., the immediate predecessor of the present incumbent of the papal chair. These we learn from his encyclical letter, bearing date September, 1832. In that letter, while lamenting the disorders and infidelity of the times, he says: "From this polluted fountain of 'indifference' flows that absurd and erroneous doctrine, or rather raving, in favor and defence of 'liberty of conscience,' for which most pestilential error the course is opened by that entire and wild liberty of opinion which is everywhere attempting the overthrow of religious and civil institutions, and which the unblushing impudence of some has held forth as an advantage to religion; hence that pest, *of all others to be dreaded in a state, unbridled liberty of opinion,* licentiousness of speech, and a lust for novelty which, according to the experience of all ages, portend the downfall of the most powerful and flourishing empires. . . . Hither tends that worst and never sufficiently to be execrated and detested *liberty of the press* for the diffusion of all

6 *

manner of writings which some so loudly contend for and so actively promote." (Appendix 3, etc.)

The pope complains also of the dissemination of unlicensed books, and, adopting the words of one of his predecessors—Clement XIII.—affirms that "no means must be here omitted, as the extremity of the case calls for all our exertions to exterminate the fatal pest which spreads through so many works; nor can the materials of error be otherwise destroyed *than by the flames*, which consume the depraved elements of the evil." After reading this, need any one be surprised at the burning of the Bible by Roman Catholics, as has been done even within these United States? It was only carrying out in practice the doctrine of the pope's letter, and "consuming the depraved elements of the evil" of which he complains, and which could not "*otherwise be destroyed than by the flames*."

When the Mexican nation formed for themselves a new constitution, about the year

1843, they inserted an article in which they profess and declare that they " will protect the Roman Apostolical Catholic religion *to the exclusion of all others.*" Provision also is made in favor of soldiers and priests in another clause, in which it is said that " the *military and ecclesiastical body* shall remain subject to *the same authorities under which they are placed by existing laws.*" These " existing laws," it is well known, exempted the persons mentioned from amenability to the civil authorities. Here, then, we have a specimen of papal liberty : no religion is tolerated or protected in the enjoyment of its privileges but the Roman Catholic, and an express provision is made that her military and ecclesiastical bodies shall not be amenable to the same laws by which other citizens are bound. And let it not be overlooked here that this exemption of the clergy from the operation of the civil laws of the country is precisely the same which was promulgated by the Third Council of Lateran in the twelfth century, and by the Fourth Council of Lateran and by Boniface VIII. in the thirteenth century, thus proving that the system of Romanism is the same in every age, and where opportunity is afforded it operates in the same intolerant form.

In closing our proof on this point, I refer, without details, to the edict of the Inquisition of Ancona against the Jews, issued by *Fra Vicenzo Salena*, the inquisitor-general of Ancona, appointed by the then reigning pontiff, Gregory XVI. By this edict the Jews were deprived of their most precious domestic, civil and religious privileges, and subjected to the severest penalties for its infraction; and as this edict is dated June 24, 1843, it cannot be excused or discredited as belonging to the dark ages. Surely, in view of these facts, the veriest skeptic must cease to doubt or to demand further proof that popery is the same now that it was in the time of Hildebrand, and that if "the penalties prescribed in the edicts of the Holy Inquisition" are not inflicted in other parts of the world than in Italy and South America, it is not for want of the will on the part of the pontiffs and their officials, but the want of power.

We have thus discussed the question in reference to the opposition of Romanism to civil and political liberty. This we have done not by loose declamation or embellished rhetoric, but by the presentation of facts and arguments, the greater part of them drawn from their own books, from the decrees of their councils, the bulls of their popes, and the acts of their official and authorized agents. From these undoubted sources we have shown you that Romanism deprives the people of the free use of the Bible, the great text-book of civil liberty, and, by doing so, saps its very foundations. We have presented to you the proof that it vests in the hands of the pope, or the pope and the general councils, a despotic and irresponsible power, altogether incompatible with the safe enjoyment of personal and public liberty. We have shown you that, by the teachings of Romanism, moral obligation is set aside, oaths and compacts disregarded, and human rights sacrificed for the benefit of the Church. We have, moreover, demonstrated that this system is intolerant and persecuting in its nature, and that now, as in former days, the opportunity and the power only are wanting to make the flames of the Inquisition the arbiters of men's opinions and the purifiers of their faith.

What impressions these statements may make on men's minds we do not know. But the subject has been discussed from a deep conviction that it is one with which American Christians and citizens should be acquainted. At the present time it is especially important to scan its nature and with watchful eye observe its progress. Special efforts are and have been making by the see of Rome and her adherents on the continent of Europe to propagate Romanism in these United

States. Immense sums of money are expended annually for this purpose. Multitudes of Roman Catholic emigrants are encouraged and aided to come over to this fair land and possess it. Jesuit priests, the faithful and well-trained officials of the pope, are constantly arriving. Bishoprics are being erected, and bishops, consecrated by pontifical hands, are placed in all our large cities to sustain the interests of Rome and to exert their influence in favor of principles which, if carried into practical effect, would subvert our liberties.

This is no idle dream, as some would have it believed. It is a living, acting reality, which, if it has not done so already, must, before very long, force itself on the attention of all. We ask our fellow-Christians to look at it, to examine its workings, and to offer up prayers to God continually that the Protestant Church and country may be led to the adoption of such moral and religious means as may most effectually stem its progress.

We ask no inquisitorial power, no infuriate mob, to aid us in withstanding the march of popery. *"The weapons of our warfare are not carnal."* It is by moral force alone that we hope to prevail. It is by the word of God, by the power of the Holy Ghost, by the administrative energy of the Lord Jesus Christ, the only Head of the Church, that we look for the destruction of this despotic power, and the establishment and triumph of pure religion and civil liberty throughout the world.